ISBN 978-0-545-32109-9

12 11 10 9 8 7 6 5   11 12 13 14 15/0

Printed in the U.S.A.   08

First Scholastic printing, December 2010

Based on "The Night Before Christmas" by Clement C. Moore

LITTLE CRITTER'S
THE NIGHT BEFORE
CHRISTMAS

BY
MERCER MAYER

SCHOLASTIC INC.
New York Toronto London Auckland
Sydney Mexico City New Delhi Hong Kong

'Twas the night before Christmas when all through the house,
Not a critter was stirring, not even a mouse.

The stockings were hung by the chimney with care,
In hopes that Santa Claus soon would be there.

We were nestled all snug in our beds,

While visions of sugarplums danced in our heads.

And Mom in her kerchief, and Dad in his cap,
Had just settled down for a long winter's nap,

When out on the lawn there arose such a clatter,
I sprang from my bed to see what was the matter.

Away to the window I flew like a flash,
Tore open the shutters and threw up the sash.

When what to my wondering eyes should appear
But an old-fashioned sleigh with eight prancing reindeer.
With a little old driver so lively and quick,
I knew in a moment it must be St. Nick.

More rapid than eagles his reindeer they came,
And he whistled and shouted and called them by name:
"Now, Dasher! Now, Dancer! Now, Prancer and Vixen!
On, Comet! On, Cupid! On, Donder and Blitzen!"

So up to the housetop the reindeer flew,
With a sleigh full of toys and Santa Claus, too.

And then in a twinkle I heard on the roof
The prancing and pawing of each little hoof.
As I drew in my head and was turning around,
Down the chimney Santa Claus came with a bound.

He was dressed all in fur from his head to his foot,
And his clothes were all tarnished with ashes and soot.
A bundle of toys he had flung on his back,
And he looked like a peddler just opening his pack.

His eyes, how they twinkled! His dimples, how merry!

His cheeks were like roses, his nose like a cherry!

His comical mouth was drawn up like a bow,

And the beard on his chin was as white as the snow.

He had a broad face and a little round belly
That shook when he laughed like a bowl full of jelly.
He was chubby and plump, a right jolly old elf.
And I laughed when I saw him, in spite of myself.

He spoke not a word but went straight to his work,
And filled all the stockings, then turned with a jerk,
And laying his finger aside of his nose
And giving a nod, up the chimney he rose.

He sprang to his sleigh, to his team gave a whistle,
And away they all flew like the down of a thistle.
But I heard him exclaim as he drove out of sight: